R185

KU-735-764

AND FINALLY...

Presented by Martyn Lewis
Illustrations by Bill Tidy

CENTURY PUBLISHING
London

First published in Great Britain by
Century Publishing Co Ltd,
Portland House, 12–13 Greek Street, London W1V 5LE

Copyright © in text Independent Television News Ltd/Martyn Lewis 1984

All rights reserved

ISBN 0 7126 9023 7

Made by Lennard Books
Mackerye End
Harpenden, Herts AL5 5DR

Editor Michael Leitch
Designed by David Pocknell's Company Ltd
Production Reynolds Clark Associates Ltd
Printed and bound in Great Britain by
Butler & Tanner Ltd, Frome, Somerset

Picture Acknowledgments
Neville Pyne p.76
Press Association pp.105, 109, 110, 114-115
UPI pp.40-41, 65

CONTENTS

Preface 7
Falling Foul 8
Record Tales 18
Tales of the Unexpected 28
Nothing Can Possibly Go Wrong . . . 44
Animal Antics 54
Excuses, Excuses 67
Time on Their Hands 73
Love and Marriage 78
Shaken and Stirred 83
Good Sports 88
Naughty but Nice 94
Difficult Deliveries 96
House Call 99
Continuing Embarrassment 102

PREFACE

"And Finally . . ."– two words in the last minute of *News At Ten* which promise at the very least the raising of an eyebrow or two, at best that a good laugh is on the way . . . part of a long-running understanding between us and you at home that even on those days when the news seems a little gloomy, we'll try our best to send you to bed with a smile.

At ITN we call this story the "Tailpiece", a kind of PS on the end of the day's news, an afterthought that has grown from its introduction in the 1950s to become an almost indispensable hallmark of all ITN news programmes. I say *almost* indispensable because occasionally it does go AWOL – squeezed out by the pressure of more important news stories on that particular day, or, just possibly, because no light story of note has emerged from the news-gathering machine. But mostly it is there – tucked away, usually briefly, like a passing encounter with an old friend – before Alastair, Sandy, Pam or I say goodnight, the closing music crowds in, and, judging from your letters, everyone wonders what on earth the two newscasters are saying to each other in that closing "two-shot" that has become a *News At Ten* trademark. Forgive me if I don't give the game away on that!

But through this book, with the help of Bill Tidy's marvellous cartoons, I *can* bring together from across the years a host of our better tailpieces, to remind you of the mad, eccentric, delightful and unexpected moments that were ITN's look at the lighter side of the news.

Martyn Lewis

FALLING FOUL

A block of flats in New York had been raided by thieves so many times that the residents put up a notice. It said quite simply: "THERE'S NOTHING LEFT TO TAKE". The thieves disagreed. Someone stole the notice!

And yet somehow New York's criminal fraternity completely missed out on one of the biggest opportunities ever likely to come their way. At five o'clock one afternoon a man walked into the famous diamond merchants Cartier's to buy a New Year gift. He had plenty to choose from – jewellery worth millions of dollars was on display throughout the six-storey building. But the customer – a lawyer – couldn't find anyone to serve him. So he telephoned the police. They discovered that all the staff had gone home early at half-past four, leaving the entire building unlocked and unattended. Luckily none of the showcases had been tampered with -- but despite this good news, the president of Cartier's didn't sleep too well that night. He later told a reporter: "Every fifteen minutes I woke up and said to myself – 'They left the front door open!'"

But even when thieves do take advantage of an open door, they don't always get it right. Someone stole 140 shoes from a parked car in Manchester, and ended up with an enormous problem – all the shoes were for left feet.

Robbers seldom return to the scene of their crime, but one bandit in Detroit has successfully broken that golden rule. He robbed the same bank no less than three times in six months. After his last raid, one of the bank clerks said: "The only difference is that each time he comes in he's a little better dressed!"

You never can judge by appearances. The candidate for the job of mayor in the town of Orange, New Jersey certainly looked respectable enough. But the local sheriff ran him into jail after

he'd shaken hands with a voter. The voter complained that during the handshake her diamond ring had disappeared. That's one way of saving your deposit.

A prosperous newspaper worker found his savings under close scrutiny after he was stopped by police in the early hours of the morning. Reginald Westrip – a member of the print union SOGAT – had on him *two* union cards, one in a false name, and *three* wage packets, two from the *Sunday Times* and one from the *Radio Times*. The judge, who said he'd been told that falsifying wage dockets was a widespread practice in Fleet Street, awarded Westrip six weeks in jail.

Sometimes, of course, the guardians of the law drop their guard when they have other things on their mind. A coach driver was fined £10 and disqualified from driving for six months for exceeding the speed limit on the M4 motorway near Reading. The court heard that when the police patrol car caught up with the coach, they discovered that it contained a rugby team on their way to a match in South Wales. The team were all members of the Metropolitan police force.

Then there was the man who couldn't have picked a worse moment to make a protest at a boxing match. During one of the bouts he dashed from his ringside seat in the Albert Hall and threw pins, needles and broken glass into the ring. He was removed shouting and screaming – and there was no problem about eye-witnesses. The audience included several thousand policemen watching the National Police Boxing Championships.

In Birmingham, another gentleman found himself out of tune with the law. Magistrates sent him to jail for a fortnight – for whistling in court. Despite repeated warnings to be quiet, he whistled on and on in the dock. The man was in court for making a nuisance of himself at home – by whistling on his balcony while all the

SENDING THE JUDGE OFF
ISN'T GOING TO HELP
YOUR CASE!

neighbours were trying to sleep.

    People standing in a bus queue in Brighton found themselves under attack – by paper clip! A man standing at an office window, shooting paper clips at the queue, was arrested after a woman complained to a police inspector that one clip had lodged in her hair. A thorough police search round the bus-stop produced another fifteen paper clips. The man, Michael Venner, was charged with "wantonly discharging a missile – to wit, a paper clip – in a public place." He pleaded guilty and was fined £2.

    Justice was certainly seen to be done in Chicago when police arrested two men for quarrelling on a train. It turned out they were both convicted pickpockets, and had started fighting when each tried to steal the other's wallet at exactly the same time.

An Idaho man had a lucky escape when a Valentine's Day quarrel with his girlfriend ended with her firing a revolver at him. The bullet was deflected by the zipper on his trousers and came out through his pocket. *He* was slightly bruised and severely shocked. *She* was charged with assault.

You'd think that if you were shot, you'd know all about it. Not so! A French housewife from Lyons woke up in the middle of the night with a violent headache. Rubbing the sore part of her head, she noticed what she thought was a slight graze – and a trace of blood. She quickly washed off the blood, dabbed on a little antiseptic, and went back to sleep beside her husband. The violent headache continued for no fewer than ten days. Doctors were mystified, prescribing a series of strong painkillers without success. Then, as a last resort, one of them recommended an X-ray. This revealed a .22 bullet lodged in her skull. Surgeons successfully removed the bullet. Under police questioning her husband confessed he'd fired a shot at her while she was asleep. He was charged with attempted murder.

Boys will be boys! But a juvenile court in London was told of one who went a shade too far. After failing an exam to join the Paras, he wandered on to an Army firing range and came across a £20,000 tank that someone had parked there. The boy said he started it up easily and played with it for three days until it ran out of fuel. His father said it made "a hell of a noise" all through the August Bank Holiday. The Army weren't too worried, though. They said it was obsolete – and they found it only a mile away from where they'd left it.

It wasn't the only time the law got tanked up about a teenage escapade. One soldier was so proud of the 50-ton Chieftain tank he'd just learnt to drive that he decided to take it home to show to Mum. So he drove it for sixty miles across Dorset and Hampshire, arriving at his Mum's front door in Basingstoke during the early hours of the

morning. Later that day, with police patrol cars in close pursuit, he took it round to show to the teachers in his old school, and parked it in the playground. The soldier's parents said they were a little surprised to see the tank – but the children at school weren't. They'd been due for a lesson on traffic control and thought the master had excelled himself.

The Welsh "leak" took on a whole new meaning before a rugby international at Twickenham, when a fan was fined for having one in a public place. He turned up at the magistrates' court dressed as a Welsh dragon – just as he was when arrested. And true to form he scored the first penalty of the day – a £10 fine for being drunk and disorderly.

A Bedouin tribesman really got the hump when he was arrested in what was then Israeli-occupied Sinai. He had "concealed about his person" a sackful of non-kosher protected lobsters. The court fined him two camels for illegal fishing – and one camel for threatening officials with a dagger. It's believed to be the first time in legal history that a man's means of transport were accepted in payment of a fine.

A Filipino woman made a strange request when a London court fined her £500 for shoplifting. Could she get a discount for cash? The magistrate was not amused. But others are more tolerant – if not downright generous. A struggling street musician, Randolph Miller, was fined £25 at Marlborough Street Magistrates' Court in London for possessing cannabis. The court was told that Miller had been arrested while playing a borrowed guitar outside Oxford Circus Tube Station. Miller went on to explain to the magistrate, Mr David Hopkins, that he'd been depressed at being unable to get a job as a musician, and took to cannabis to cheer himself up. He'd put down £10 on a second-hand guitar, but couldn't afford the rest. Mr Hopkins was so touched by the story that he awarded Miller the £65 he needed to buy the guitar out of a special court fund. It wasn't the first time Mr Hopkins had been so generous... three years earlier he awarded another busker a 75 pence tin flute to stop him begging.

Not all defendants get such gentle treatment. In Chicago a circuit court judge, faced with a man who was hurling things about the court, jumped over the bench and pinned him to the floor. The judge was an ex-football player. The defendant was upset because he'd been ordered to see a psychiatrist.

Another – and even more novel – way of clearing a court was discovered in South Africa. No sooner had the defendant, who'd been charged with theft, stepped into the dock than he produced a four-foot brown snake. The courtroom emptied within seconds, the complainant and all witnesses disappeared, and the magistrate had to postpone the hearing.

More often than not it's the judges who give the defendant a bad time – especially if he just happens to be a one-legged burglar with a glass eye and a deformed hand. A man answering to that description was sentenced to 90 days' community service at York Crown Court. The judge followed up the sentence by offering some unsolicited advice as well. He told Philip McCutcheon: "You're a rotten burglar. Whoever heard of a burglar succeeding with one leg, something wrong with his hand, and a glass eye. Don't you think it's time you gave up crime?"

That judge would have had little luck with 27-year-old Charles Henry Kensett, an incorrigible rogue who was sent to London Sessions for sentence. A detective told the court that Kensett's one ambition was to go back to prison. Asked why, the detective said: "He tells me they have good cowboy films in prison around Christmas time." Kensett got twelve months – so at least he was sure of one more good Christmas.

A convict serving 18 months for a firearms offence at Incesu in Turkey found a novel way of getting his own back. He bought the jail for about £6,000, and said he wouldn't be renewing the prison's lease when it ran out. Instead, he'd be setting up in business making sausages when he got out. His final comment: "I feel really at home now."

A convicted killer at Lewes Prison in Sussex created a home too – but one that was strictly for the birds. He built a bird sanctuary alongside the prison exercise yard, and people started sending injured and sick birds to him for treatment. The last we heard, the Lewes birdman – serving a life sentence – had plans to expand and give the birds more room to fly.

Traffic warden Willie Walker certainly gave motorists plenty of room in his home town of Dumfries. When he retired it was revealed that he'd only issued five parking tickets during his entire 17-year career – and only then because a policeman ordered him to do so.

When a new law requiring drivers and front-seat passengers to wear seatbelts came into force in Britain, it wasn't long before it claimed its first casualty. George Statham, who weighs 27 stone, announced he was giving up driving because he couldn't find a seat belt long enough to go round him. Rather than face a £50 fine for not belting up, George decided that if it was a straight choice between giving up food or giving up the keys to his van, then it was the van that had to go.

More food for thought in an unusual road accident in Suffolk. The scene – a narrow, winding country lane, with a van and a car travelling fast in opposite directions. A crash was inevitable – they collided head-on, and the car was a write-off. Luckily no-one was seriously hurt, but as the two drivers got out to remonstrate with each other they got another shock. They were husband and wife! In the van – Mr Matthew Stephenson. In the car – his wife Margaret. Those whom God hath joined together...

And finally – in Chicago – a man charged with nine traffic offences had the case dismissed through lack of evidence. His name? Mr Guilty.

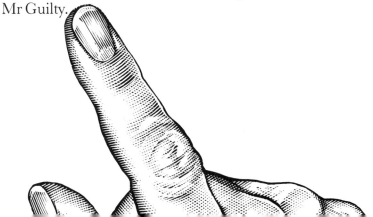

RECORD TALES

To say you're attempting a world record will prick up the ears of even the most indolent of newsdesks, and there was a period in the Sixties and early Seventies when curious and ingenious contests were even more in vogue than they are now. Some weren't exactly headline-grabbers – but they dominated the closing thirty seconds of *News At Ten*.

Rag students from Glasgow claimed a new record for cramming – not, alas, for exams, but to see how many people they could cram into a car. No fewer than 40 girls squeezed their way into a Humber Hawk saloon. To the relief of the manufacturers, it didn't catch on.

At Hampton Grammar School's fête, 65 boys piled onto a single bed to claim another world record. They agreed that 67 American airmen had done the same thing earlier, but said that didn't count because the airmen used a specially made bed. At the United States base at Ruislip, a sergeant said they wouldn't take the challenge lying down.

There's not a lot you can do with beds – except in America where they *race* them. This unusual sporting craze took off to such an extent that they staged the world's first bed-racing championship in Unionville, Missouri. Each bed was allowed a "crew" of five – four pushers and one driver – racing over a specially designed course. Forty beds competed for the title in front of a crowd of three thousand excited bed-racing fans. This is one sport where they might be forgiven for falling asleep – but nobody did, least of all the man who set a new world record (they said) by riding a bed up a ramp to jump 16 feet over a sack of rattlesnakes.

If you're wondering how the snakes got into the sack – well, in America that's a national sport too. Thousands of fans turn up every year – usually in Texas – to watch the experts being put through their

paces down in the pits. The big prizes go to anyone who gets ten snakes into one sack without flinching or falling.

A student at California University claimed a new world record after completing 1,151 revolutions in a large spin-drier. Laurence Scanlon's "journey" took 28 minutes – and friends held the drier door slightly open to prevent over-heating. Scanlon described himself as a "laundronaut".

An even more bizarre world record – for staying underground – was claimed by Mike Costello at Belle Vue in Manchester. A former "human cannonball" known professionally as "Blondini", he stayed in a glass-topped coffin for 78 days 1 hour 5 minutes without a break. Visitors paid ten pence a time to gaze at him lying in his tomb. "Perhaps," he commented, "some of them were depressed, and

seeing my circumstances made them a little happier."

American Bruce McLaughlin was really up in the clouds when he broke a record that is under constant assault. He made no fewer than 235 parachute jumps in 24 hours.

The world's shortest scheduled airline flight is claimed by Loganair who operate small aircraft in the Highlands and Islands of

Scotland. One of their planes takes off from the island of Westray in the Orkney Islands, and lands on another island – Papa Westray – a mere 58 seconds later. That's about as long as it takes to read from the start of this chapter. The price is £9 – and no – it doesn't include a meal!

It's not often you hear of the police claiming a record. But way down in New Orleans they've arrested the same man 820 times. He's been convicted 421 times – mostly for being drunk in public. The name of this habitual offender was Alfred L. Vice.

The world domino-toppling record has fallen. West German Klaus Friedrich set up seven miles of dominoes – three hundred thousand in all. They took a full ten minutes to fall – and knocked spots off the previous record which they beat by nearly a mile.

Ralph Weetering had a hero's welcome when he arrived back home in Melbourne, Australia with a most prestigious trophy. Ralph, who worked for the local fire brigade, was the new world whistling champion. He outwhistled an international field of over three thousand at Carson City, Nevada to take the cup – itself shaped like a whistle – from the United States.

There is not much international competition for one of Turkey's favourite sports. Local man Hussein Cokal won their national grease-wrestling championship – no mean feat when you think how easy it would have been for victory to just slip from his grasp.

He wouldn't have been much of an opponent for Southampton student John Apostolou who claimed a world handshaking record. He shook hands 15,800 times in just seven hours – which is an average of 37 times a minute. You can't really call it sport – but at least it's friendly.

A meal and a half won 20-year-old technology student Dick Baxter a new world record – for sausage eating. At Matlock Bath in Derbyshire he devoured 96 inches of sausage to beat the old record by a mere two inches – or half a sausage.

Thirty-one-year-old Scotsman John Kenmuir kept his world haggis-eating title by devouring a pound and a half of warm haggis in 74 seconds. He wasn't quite as fast as the previous year – but confessed that this time he'd had too many chips for tea.

Twenty-four-year-old Tony Norton, from London, won a £250 holiday in Switzerland when he retained his title of world champion needle threader. In the finals at Manchester he put 1,171 threads through the eye of a rug needle in two hours – a darned clever achievement.

Mr Harold Soden of New York laid claim to the world pipe-smoking championship. Sixteen competitors gathered for the contest. Each was allowed sixty seconds to get his pipe going, only two matches and one fill of tobacco. Mr Soden managed to keep puffing his one fill for 1 hour 10 minutes 15 seconds.

A diamond called the Polar Star came under the hammer in Geneva and fetched almost two million pounds. Once owned by Napoleon's brother, it weighed over 41 carats – which made it a world record per carat as well as for a single stone. After its Bonaparte period it belonged to a Russian princess and finally to Lady Deterding, wife of the founder of Royal Dutch Shell. Its new owner, Mr Razeen Saliah of Sri Lanka, paid £1,960,784. He said he'd bought it as an investment.

They were rather more down to earth in Ashington in North-east England when growers gathered in a working men's club to try and find the world's heaviest onion. The rules were tough – Mr Rogers, a farm worker from Fife, was forced to cut off the top of his vegetable before weighing. But he still won first prize – a cheque for £500. His onion had a girth of $25\frac{1}{2}$ inches, and weighed in at a mighty 6 lb 7 oz.

Tellers of tall stories – which, we hope, don't include any you've been reading here – were due at a Lake District pub to compete for the title "Biggest Liar in the World". Entries were promised from as far away as America and Australia, but the organizers weren't sure how many would turn up. Some of the entrants, you see, were less than truthful about their intentions. Those who did arrive found a scrupulously well organized competition – to make it fair on everyone they banned politicians and lawyers.

There comes a point in every failed record attempt when you have to give up. Michael Briggs's moment of resignation came after six years of living in a tent in a bid to set a new world record for sleeping out of doors. Michael, from Somerset, was thirteen when he first pitched camp in his back garden, and over the years he wore out eleven tents and eight sleeping bags. So why zip up the tent for good after more than two thousand nights and six winters? Michael blamed intense competition from America, where some campers have already been out for nine years.

Second mate Bill Neal, from Plymouth, crossed the Channel in – of all things – his bath. And because the French can get difficult about letting anyone land from something they don't like the look of, Bill had his bath – complete with taps – registered at Lloyd's as an "ocean-going craft". It was powered by one oar and Bill's strong left arm. The voyage took him $13\frac{1}{2}$ hours. Luckily, no-one else wanted to use the bath.

Howard Blakely from Florida found that his garden was getting him down. With acres of grass to cut he found most of the regular lawnmowers a little short on staying power. So he decided to build one himself. He used part of the body of a burned-out Volkswagen Beetle, an air-conditioning engine from a Greyhound bus, a treadle iron frame and the wheels from two golf carts. But he's still not entirely satisfied. He says the next one must have air conditioning for the driver. Even so – that's one beetle that goes down well in the garden.

Mrs Daisy Farrington had one great unfulfilled ambition. She wanted to fly – just once – in an aeroplane. On her hundredth birthday friends and relatives clubbed together to make sure her wish was granted. A smart car complete with motorcycle escort turned up at the old people's home at Ladywood in Birmingham to whisk her away to the airport. There Great-Granny Farrington squeezed into the co-pilot's seat of a Piper Cherokee – and the lady who was just a lass when man took to the air for the first time lifted off on her very

first flight. She gave the thumbs
up from the cockpit and said
afterwards that it had been a
great experience – and she
wouldn't mind doing it again.

And finally, while Mrs
Farrington had to wait a long
time for *her* big chance, four
women bridge players found
theirs a little more quickly.
Playing a game in California,
they were each dealt a complete
suit. According to statistics this is
only supposed to happen once every
sixty-two million million years. And
the odds against it happening at all are
about two and a quarter million, million,
million, million to one.

TALES OF THE UNEXPECTED

A man – rather hard up for cash – walked into a pawn shop in Tucson, Arizona with what he claimed were his sole remaining assets . . . three choice T-bone steaks. After due negotiation the owner offered him six dollars and promised to hold the steaks for thirty days in a freezer in the back of his shop. He said that if the man didn't come back he'd eat his assets for lunch.

A Cornish fishmonger, Jim Sullivan from Liskeard, who'd had a bellyfull of his local council, decided to bite back after they refused to let him open a fish and chip takeaway in a corner of his shop. When a rates bill arrived for £222 he wrote out a cheque on the underbelly of a 350-pound shark – and delivered it to the council treasurer's department. After some deliberation the council accepted the cheque, but had to use a van to pay it into the bank. Jim said he was happy – he'd made his point.

A driving examiner went to court to make his. And got £8,000 and costs from two drivers he tested. A district nurse, Mrs Bessie Millar, reversed so violently that the examiner badly twisted his neck. Another lady gave him a hernia when she drove into a wall.

On the other hand, being a learner is no fun either. A pub landlady from Exeter took 23 years to pass her driving test. Betty Tudor was such a nervous driver she was banned by no fewer than three driving schools – and one of them even went so far as to refuse to teach her sister, just because they were related. However, after three hundred lessons, Betty finally made it, and hung up her L-plates for good. But while she was delighted, several thousand other motorists in Exeter weren't so sure.

Mrs Kay Creasey and her husband, from Lincoln, were on honeymoon in Torquay when they found a gold bracelet lost by a Viking a thousand years ago. Mrs Creasey said her husband hadn't wanted to go for a walk on the beach, but she'd insisted, and when

ERIC THE BEIGE... HE'S LOST HIS GOLD BRACELET SOMEWHERE!

she noticed the bracelet in the sand he said: "Don't be silly, that's not gold." The bracelet was sold at Sotheby's for £6,500. The couple kissed and made up – and put down the cash as a deposit on a new house. An elderly couple spent most of their lives just inches away from another windfall. Every night, as they went to sleep, one of them would reach out and switch off a lightbulb stuck in an old vase. Then the man from Sotheby's called round to value some other stuff and recognized the vase as a 14th-century Chinese bottle. At auction it fetched £290,000. Just as well they didn't drill a hole in it for an electric wire. That would have reduced its value to a mere £145,000.

Norman and Anne Hartas, from North Yorkshire, were expecting a few thousand pounds when they sent an old painting on a firescreen to London for auction. It turned out to be a work by the 16th-century artist Hans Hoffman – and it fetched a cool £370,000.

Then there was the mystery of the missing punter who won

£100,000 for a stake of just £1.43. He backed seven different horses to win in a series of doubles, trebles and accumulators. The odds against him succeeding were two million to one. But it was a full two days before George Talbot, a retired docker from Portsmouth, got round to collecting his winnings. He said he'd been too busy baby-sitting with his grandchildren to check the results.

In April 1981, a Californian man walked into the Flamingo Hilton in Las Vegas to have a quiet flutter on the slot machines. He'd been playing for about twenty minutes and was down to his last ten dollars when he got a row of five sevens and the machine rang every bell it had. The payout was a world record – $355,000.

But that record didn't stand for long. Exactly three months later to the day Jeff Randolph won nearly $1 million from a slot machine in Lake Tahoe, Nevada. He'd lost $23 in ten minutes when four triple bars clicked into place. Randolph, who's single, said: "If I listened to the girls here tonight, I'd be married tomorrow."

He'd probably spent the money by the time the record was broken again. Still in Nevada – a year and a half later – 63-year-old Rocco Dinublo, a grape grower from California, won two and a half million dollars from a fruit machine – that's getting on for two million British pounds at today's prices.

There is another little-known way to become a millionaire – as a Chinese pilot found when he defected to Taiwan in an ancient Soviet fighter. He only just made it – the plane landed with enough fuel left for one more minute's flying. The Taiwan government called an immediate press conference to announce that the pilot had got the standard advertised reward – a Chinese takeaway of over a million pounds in gold.

Easy come, easy go, too. A London court ordered an Arab gambler to pay £1,500,000 in gambling debts, interest and costs. Mr Shehadeh Twal lost it in Mayfair in just four hours – almost more than all the members of OPEC made between them in that time.

A Chesterfield doctor got a fright when his monthly bank

statement showed him overdrawn by just a penny under £10 million.
The bank told him not to worry – it was just a computer error.

The Glasgow *Daily Record* found itself shelling out more than it
bargained for when it ran a holiday contest. The prize was a two-
week holiday in Italy plus £50 a head spending money for the
winning family. They turned out to be Mr Joseph Kennedy, his wife
Bridget, and their *fifteen* children!

Britain's electricity moguls cast themselves more in the role of
Scrooge when a poor pensioner appealed to them for help. For ten
years Mrs Dorothy Culley allowed them to hang their cables across
her front garden in Yorkshire, and for ten years they paid her exactly
the same sum in return – $2\frac{1}{2}$ pence a year, paid by cheque. She said
that was really too little – what with inflation and all that. So the
Electricity Board upped the rent – to 3p a year.

A group of insurance brokers found an unusual way of saving
money – by building a runway on a racecourse. An executive jet
made an emergency landing on Mallow race track in Ireland. But
short of dismantling it, there was no way it could take off again. It
turned out to be cheaper to build a full-scale runway at the
racecourse than pay out the insurance money on the plane.

More financial help came from the workers of Delta Airlines in
America. They raised $30 million – not for themselves, but as a
present for their management. They used the money to buy a brand
new Boeing 767 passenger jet and gave it to the airline. "They took
good care of us," one worker said. "Now we want to take care of
them."

ITN's industrial correspondent Michael Green found he
wasn't as well looked after as usual when he popped into a sale at
Harrods to buy a pair of trousers. While he was trying them on, his
own trousers disappeared. It turned out that an over-enthusiastic
assistant had sold them by mistake.

One of the advantages of sitting behind a desk in the studio is
that no-one knows whether you're wearing trousers or not.

Fortunately Harrods did not pursue this line of argument, and Michael's dignity was soon restored ... along with a new pair of trousers.

Policemen in the West German city of Bonn once had their own bare-legged adventure. It got so hot during a heatwave that officers on point duty outside the Parliament building were allowed to roll up their trousers and stand barefoot in buckets of water. However, to stop people laughing at them, screens were placed around them up to the knees.

A Belgian artist, Jean Verame, spent six months on a most unusual project – he painted eleven million square feet of the Sinai desert a bright blue, and planned to cover other parts black, red and yellow, until conservationists and politicians began to protest. It seemed it had all been a misunderstanding. Officials had given permission for the man "to paint the Sinai desert". And when it was actually announced like that in the press, everyone thought that the government was commissioning a series of canvases of that famous piece of territory. How wrong can you be?

And whoever would have thought that there'd be a litter problem on the world's highest mountain – Mount Everest. But that's exactly what happened. Over the years, as one expedition followed another, the pile of discarded equipment – from food to empty oxygen bottles – has grown steadily. Now Nepal is insisting that all expeditions hire an extra ten porters to cart away the rubbish. One climber said that some abandoned camps looked like department stores.

Mr Thomas Bridson didn't need a base camp for his mountaineering expedition. On the spur of the moment he decided to climb two thousand feet up Snaefell in the Isle of Man, and sing *John Peel* when he got to the top. Mr Bridson was just a few weeks off his hundredth birthday!

British industry – which doesn't always get a good press – can provide plenty of testimonials to its ingenuity. The CBI has revealed

that British firms are selling refrigerators to the Eskimos, canned Scottish loch water to the Americans, false eyelashes to the Soviet Union, French 'antique' furniture (made in Britain!) to France, and sand to Egypt and Saudi Arabia. And in San Francisco you could at one time buy tins of pure English country air – at about fifty pence each!

Thieves used a crane to steal a fibreglass cesspool from a farm near Maidstone in Kent. They pounced the night before the £2,500 cesspool, weighing almost three-quarters of a ton, was due to be installed. A police spokesman confirmed that they were on the scent.

Mr Tim Hardy, who spreads muck for Her Majesty on her estate at Sandringham, applied for a Royal Warrant to be "muckspreader by appointment to the Queen". Three years went by, and Mr Hardy thought his request had fallen on deaf ears. But just when he'd given up all hope of receiving the accolade, the Royal Warrant arrived. Now he proudly displays the royal crest on his entire fleet of muckspreaders.

Sedgemoor District Council in Somerset came up with an earthy wedding present for Prince Charles and Lady Diana. They decided to give them a ton of peat, worth £127, for their garden. The council reckoned that the peat, produced locally, would be more useful than a lot of other presents that might end up in the basement of Buckingham Palace.

A pretty little girl jumped up on Santa Claus's lap in a shop in Springfield, Missouri. She rubbed her cheek against his whiskers, gave him a great big kiss and whispered in his ear: "Know what I've got?" "No," said Santa. The little girl replied: "The mumps."

A Norwegian fishing trawler reported an ususual catch. When the 950-ton ship was fishing in the Barents Sea it felt a violent tug on its trawl wire, and was then pulled backwards at full speed. It had netted a 300-foot submarine. The crew of the unmarked sub sheepishly sent over a boarding party to cut their tail fins free.

Chief Officer Francis Schremp, of the American freighter *John*

Lykes, was washed overboard by a 50-foot wave during an Atlantic crossing. As he couldn't swim, he thought he was a goner. But the next wave – also a 50-footer – picked him up again and deposited him back on the deck, badly bruised and shaken. As he acted as the ship's doctor, he had to treat his own injuries for the rest of the voyage.

Six giant crabs were on their way by air from Alaska to zoos in London, Manchester and Hamburg when a chef spotted them in the airliner's cold room. Not knowing how rare they were, he popped them in the oven and served them up to the delighted passengers. The zoo owners were not so pleased.

Rather more effort went into saving the toads of Wales. Scores of nature enthusiasts turned out on a busy road through Llandrindod Wells in an attempt to stop thousands of the tiny hoppers becoming road-accident victims. Once a year the toads make the journey in darkness from woodlands across the road to a lake to spawn. On this occasion wellwishers helped them across in buckets after first erecting road signs to warn motorists. "Slow, Major Toad Ahead", no doubt.

In Little Silver, New Jersey the driver of a van walked away with only minor injuries when she hit a telegraph pole. Who owned the van? The Institute of Safe Driving.

A Baltimore newspaper editor said he wasn't interested when someone phoned him with a story about a lorry rolling down a hill and crashing into a house. The caller said: "I'm glad you're taking it so calmly. It was your house!"

The Thames Television series *Danger UXB* about wartime bomb disposal made a man in Kent realize that a wartime relic he had on his bedroom wall was an unexploded "butterfly bomb". He took it to a sandpit over the road, the police evacuated 75 people from homes nearby, and Royal Engineers blew it up. Mr John Arnold, who had slept underneath it for a year, said: "I thought it was a dud – my mother often dusted it."

For two months in 1982, the government of Pakistan banned the throwing of snowballs in the small town of Muree. Anyone who got into a snowball fight faced a heavy fine, or even prison. And all because a snowball fight between students the year before had got out of hand. It must have been quite a battle!

The mayor of Capri proved he was just as responsive to

another problem. He banned the wearing of wooden-soled sandals in the streets because foreign tourists complained of the noise they made.

And finally, something else was afoot at a scientific conference in Mozambique. Delegates heard an alarming report on the damage that can be caused by high-heeled shoes. According to one of the experts present they first cause stooping shoulders and a curved back. And if that hasn't put you off wearing them, they will eventually cause wrinkles on the face. It's better than blaming old age!

NOTHING CAN POSSIBLY GO WRONG ...

oliticians and bureaucrats have their "And Finally" moments
too! Sometimes they wish the ground would open up and
swallow them, sometimes they don't notice the joke – which makes
it even funnier – and sometimes they join in the laughter with the rest
of us. But there was one story which remains, without doubt, the
most famous and controversial *News At Ten* tailpiece of all time. It was
delivered by the late Reggie Bosanquet in his inimitable style. Aware
of its potential sensitivity, ITN's editor-in-chief ordered Reggie to
read it without even a trace of a smile flickering across his face.

It was a story that came out of the firemen's nationwide strike
in the mid 1970s. Green Goddesses – the famous fire engines that
saved Britain from even more destruction during the Second World
War blitz – were brought out of mothballs, and, manned by Army
personnel, did their best to provide an emergency service. When the
strike was over the Ministry of Defence prepared a report on the
operation which included some typical incidents experienced by the
Army crews. On one occasion they had been summoned out to an
old lady's house. Her cat, which she loved dearly, had got stuck up a
tree. It was a simple job for the Army team to run up a ladder and
rescue the trapped moggie. The old lady was so overcome with
gratitude that she asked the entire crew to come in for tea and scones.
Half an hour later, they emerged with the old lady's thanks still
ringing in their ears, jumped into the Green Goddess, reversed down
the driveway – and ran over the cat!

The nation was irreparably split! Judging from the hundreds
of phone calls that poured in to ITN House – far more than on any
other occasion, before or since – half the country thought it was the
most tasteless story they had ever heard, and the other half were

clearly rolling round on the floor convulsed with laughter. Reggie
swore he'd played a straight bat – not a trace of a smile. A replay
showed he was right. But the cat lovers remained unconvinced.
ITN's tailpiece writers soldiered on – perhaps rather more warily
than before.

In February 1982 the British government published a White
Paper aimed at saving the public purse millions of pounds by cutting
out unnecessary forms. Research had shown that a staggering two
billion forms were sent out every year – the equivalent of 36 for every
man, woman and child in the country. The White Paper aimed to cut
that figure by a relatively modest five million during the first year. It
was hailed as "one-up for the little man or woman against the great
bureaucratic machine". Then at a government press conference a kit
explaining the White Paper was handed out. It ran to about two
hundred pages, weighed about two pounds, and took several hours to
read!

Bureaucrats and managers often complain that life is just one round of meetings after another. The Indian Prime Minister Mrs Ghandi grasped that particular nettle. She ordered the entire Indian Civil Service to have "one meetingless day every week, so that they can actually do some work".

Some committees work rather more profitably than others. With the American Defence budget running at $187,000 million a year, a Senate committee was given the job of looking into possible overcharging by some contractors. Of particular interest were small antenna wrenches for which the contractor was asking $9,500 – each! Senate investigators said that similar wrenches could be bought at any old hardware store for just 12 cents. Even in the Defence business, a mark-up of 80,000 per cent takes some beating.

At the other end of the scale, British financial watchdogs discovered one of the lowest returns ever from an investment. A government committee on public spending found that a toll-bridge across the River Cart at Paisley in Scotland cost the taxpayer £18,000 a year to run. Over the previous three years it had earned exactly 80 pence.

Some items are so important you can't even begin to put a value on them. That same committee on public spending once published a series of open questions to the senior civil servant at the Ministry of Defence. It asked him about vast surplus stocks of Women's Royal Army Corps underclothing, including what were called "women's pants, woollen, long". One MP said it appeared the Army had enough women's pants, woollen, long to last eight hundred years. The Defence official didn't entirely agree, but admitted there was an enormous surplus. The pants were put on the market. It's not known how many were sold – or to whom.

Japanese workers took 19 years to complete the longest tunnel in the world. Thirty-three miles long, it linked the northern island of Hokkaido to the main Japanese island, Honshu. The Prime Minister himself pressed the button to blast away the last remaining section of rock. The tunnel cost £1.3 billion to build, and the plan was to run express trains through it at 130 miles an hour. But over the years that plan changed, and the express train project was abandoned. The last we heard they were talking of using the tunnel to grow mushrooms. No doubt they'd make a profit out of that too!

MAYBE IF WE RUSHED THE
MUSHROOM SOUP HERE BY
EXPRESS TRAIN IT WOULDN'T
BE SO—— COLD!

A British Minister of Agriculture – whose name we will avoid mentioning here to spare his blushes – once threw out a challenge to chocolate manufacturers. He asked them to produce "silent wrappings" for their chocolates – so that people could go to the cinema and listen to films without being disturbed by the rustling of sweet papers.

A New York jury commissioner got quite a shock when Socrates Lovinger appeared in his office. Socrates had just received a letter summoning him for jury service, and was obediently reporting for duty. There were two problems. Socrates was just nine years old. He was also a dog.

There *are* some job opportunities for dogs. The City Water Board in Sydney, Australia, once offered several permanent appointments to suitable dogs. The only qualification was that they shouldn't be more than six inches high. They were wanted as pipe cleaners – for pulling lines through fouled pipes. The Water Board said the system would save hundreds of pounds. The city's dachshunds were, for once, walking tall!

As late as 1970 a man was excommunicated by a Jerusalem religious court for possessing "a defiling and disgusting object". People in the extreme Orthodox area of Mea Shearim were forbidden to eat, drink or sit with the man until the object was removed. Before your imagination runs wild you should know that the object in question was – a television set!

Television pictures were somewhat thin on the ground in Zambia towards the end of 1981 – but for a different reason. Zambian Television announced that until further notice it would not be covering events attended by Opposition politicians, only those at which President Kaunda was present. Embarrassed officials said there was no bias in this – it was simply that they only had three reels of unused film (about forty minutes' worth) to last them over the following three months. It is not known if the President made shorter speeches as a result.

The Soviet leader Mr Khrushchev took a fairly robust approach to what, for him, was that new-fangled thing called television. When interviewed by an American television company he refused to wear any make-up. He didn't say why himself, but officials at the Kremlin later explained: "Comrade Khrushchev shaves every day and uses talcum powder – so make-up is not necessary."

Some interpreters aren't necessary either. President Carter changed his rapidly after he mistranslated two phrases from the President's speech. "When I left the United States ..." became "When I left never to return." And "I have come to understand your desires for the future" became "I have a carnal desire for the Poles." The charitable explanation is that the interpreter was using 19th-century Polish. The White House say he came "highly recommended". The only question is: by whom?

Christmas 1977 saw the Americans and the Russians cooperating for once – to find a rather special Polar bear. She was pregnant, had a radio transmitter around her neck, and had strayed across the Bering Straits into the Soviet Union from Alaska. She was soon tracked down – by satellite.

Another bear – a Koala – got quite a mauling at the unlikely hands of Australia's Minister for Tourism. Mr John Brown said that the little creature, which features in nearly all Australia's tourist brochures, wasn't cuddly or lovely at all. "When people pick it up," he said, "they find it's flea-ridden, it piddles on you, it stinks and it scratches."

The scientists of America's National Geographic Society reached another decision of vital general interest. After studying all the evidence available, they worked out that the zebra is a light-coloured animal with dark stripes, and *not* a dark coloured animal with light stripes.

If you sometimes think that the world of politics lacks people of stature, you'd have found an ally in President Kennedy. He once ordered a new car for the White House – with an electric lift built under the rear seat. The lift was needed, apparently, because some distinguished foreign visitors in the past had been too short to see out of the car windows!

Politicians do move in mysterious ways! Three deputies were standing outside the National Assembly building in Paris during a time of fairly lively protests. A policeman told them to move on. They said that they were Members of Parliament. The policeman replied: "Move on all the same – you've done enough damage as it is."

Britain's MPs once saw the writing on the wall – their own wall – at the public entrance to the House of Commons. What were described as "hearts and love messages" were carved in the stonework. One MP described it as "the work of juvenile members of the community". Another recalled a remark attributed to Lord Curzon: "The only result of popular education," he said, "is that the rude words written on my door are written six inches lower down."

The former Prime Minister Harold Macmillan, opening a new library at Gray's Inn, told a story about Lord Birkenhead – the famous F.E. Smith – when he was Lord Chancellor. Lord Birkenhead had gone to speak at a public meeting, but was forced to sit through an extremely long and boring speech by the chairman. Eventually the chairman said: "I now call upon Lord Birkenhead to give his address." The noble Lord rose to his feet and said: "30, Grosvenor Gardens." Then he left the hall.

President Reagan has always reckoned that you can tell a lot about a person's character by the way they eat jellybeans. (These have been the President's favourite sweets ever since he stopped smoking.) As a $3\frac{1}{2}$-ton truckload of jellybeans was rushed to the White House at the start of his Presidency, Mr Reagan said the person to watch was someone who picked out only jellybeans of one colour. He didn't say why, but it's enough to make visiting politicians quite nervous about the jellybean jar.

Mrs Thatcher had something else to get nervous about when she went electioneering in London's East End. Mr Lew Pickle, who has a fruit stall in Petticoat Lane, rushed up and kissed her. Asked why, he replied: "For the novelty ... after 32 years of married life you need a change."

And finally, in the uncertain world of politics, it came as something of a blow to discover that Big Ben – that world-famous symbol of political stability – was officially leaning. By all of nine inches, to be exact. Was he leaning to the left or to the right? "Well," our Political Correspondent said cautiously, "that depends on which way you look at him." And he looked all right at the start of the News (if not at the start of this book!).

ANIMAL ANTICS

As a nation the British are potty about animals. So it's hardly surprising that quite a few of the "And Finally" pieces have concerned the tricks and escapades that animals get up to – with or without their owners.

Peter, a ship's cat, was rescued a full nine days after he and his ship sank in the River Rhine. When the wreck was raised Peter was found exhausted – but alive – in an air bubble.

Another feline who used up most of its nine lives in one go was Sedgewick, the black and white cat that blacked out most of Cambridge for several hours by strolling into an electricity transformer. He suffered a 33,000-volt shock – and was found wandering around in a somewhat dazed fashion by his worried owner. Sedgewick is now licking his wounds – he had severe burns and a leg injury – and vets say it's a wonder he survived. At any rate there's general agreement that such a hair-raising experience brought him within a whisker of death.

Lofty, a ginger tom, held up important demolition work for a day by climbing a 150-foot chimney in Bolton and refusing to come down. Fred Dibnah, the steeplejack, used every trick in the book to try to persuade the mad moggie to come down – but to no avail. The RSPCA made little impression either and the fire brigade's ladder was too short. Eventually, while everyone was at lunch, an animal-loving mountaineer called Gerry Rogers shinned up the ladder and made Lofty an offer he couldn't refuse – a firm hand on the scruff of the neck. Safely down to earth again, Lofty showed little sign of shame at making such a nuisance of himself. He basked in the glow of the photographers' flashlights – and ate three meals in one go.

Another high-flier made a surprise appearance, 30,000 feet up. The pilot of a Swissair jet flying from Chicago to Zurich kept hearing a noise that sounded like a cat miaowing. When the plane landed,

after a journey of 11,500 miles, the crew searched the plane. In the air-conditioning system they found a real cool cat – a six-month-old kitten, hungry, but unharmed.

And a cat called Wanton Bacon turned up at London's Heathrow Airport after travelling 8,500 miles from the remote Pacific island of Guam. What made that journey particularly unusual was that, according to airline staff, to make it at all he must have changed planes in Washington!

Normally cats don't take kindly to being separated from the territory they know and love. Three-year-old Ginger arrived at his old home in Perth after *walking* 250 miles from his new home in Albany on Australia's south coast. At least they think he walked – but they're checking the airline passenger lists just in case.

Cows get homesick too. When Daisy the Friesian was sold at auction at Okehampton in Devon, she was parted from her baby calf. She missed the calf so much she jumped a gate, trotted six miles across country, through woods and along lanes, until she found it. Daisy's new owner, Bob Woolacot from Exbourne in Devon, said he would never have thought it possible. And just to give the story a happy ending, he bought the calf as well.

More conventional, but no less remarkable, was the incredible journey of Sam the mongrel dog. His owners sold him when they moved from Montrose in Colorado to Santee, California – but ten weeks later he turned up at their new home. Sam had followed his nose for 840 miles across four states. He was weak, hungry, and dog-tired of course, but made a quick recovery. Sam's owner, Ray Foltz, was so impressed he decided Sam could stay.

Dogs can be most loyal creatures – and South Carolina police found that out the hard way. Searching for an escaped convict they sent their bloodhound ahead to try and pick up the man's footprints. Then they noticed that the tracks of the dog were running side by side with those of the hunted man. It turned out that the convict used to feed it in prison. The search for man *and* dog continued.

Dogs can also mean big trouble. America produced a headline not of "Man bites dog" but "Dog shoots man". Mr John Calbert bought an Alsatian guard dog which he called Jarvis. He was training him to attack and disarm intruders – but Jarvis didn't get it quite right. He picked up Mr Calbert's loaded .22 pistol and dropped it. It went off, shooting Mr Calbert in the arm. He was in hospital in Monroe, Michigan. Jarvis was in the doghouse.

Who would want a slightly arthritic 11-year-old English Setter

called Patti? Her 74-year-old owner made sure in her will that someone would. The lady, who'd inherited a family fortune, never married and had no surviving relatives. So when she died she left a quarter of a million pounds to a Manchester doctor, Alva Brown, on the strict condition that he took good care of Patti.

Seventy-five-year old Leyton Orfield from Minneapolis has an unusual hobby – he trains pigs just like dogs. And he does such a good job that even some dogs can't tell the difference. Every morning he puts his latest pig Rudi on a lead and takes him for a walk. And once a week the pair of them turn up at the local dog obedience class. Mr Orfield says that pigs are quicker on the uptake than dogs and generally much smarter than people think. With friends like Mr Orfield, it's hardly surprising that some little piggies like to stay at home!

Some big piggies too. A Californian family have a pet boar that weighs in at around four hundred pounds. They allow it to wander freely round the house – sneak into the kitchen for an occasional biscuit – and even stretch out beside the fire in the lounge.

Another pig really in the swim of things was spotted by five fishermen off the Florida coast. Their boat was fifteen miles out to sea when they noticed a pig having a swim. No-one knows how he got there, but the fishermen threw out a net and quickly hauled in their unlikely catch. They said he was a bit sunburned and encrusted in salt, but apart from that seemed very pleased to see them. He drank a lot of fresh water, had a meal, and then went to sleep.

Animals often take it into their heads to do the craziest things. A normally placid Pyrenean Mountain dog called Rollo developed an unusual appetite – for car wing mirrors. As cars slowed down to negotiate the bend close to his home, Rollo would leap out and savage the mirror – leaving bemused or angry motorists to carry on their way with a trail of broken glass behind them. Rollo cost his West Country owner hundreds of pounds in compensation. But his biggest problem was that he thought the wing mirrors on police panda cars tasted best.

Tina, a Jack Russell terrier, thought she was a cat – and developed a strange passion for climbing trees. She made it all look incredibly easy, and enjoyed it so much she even gave up going for walks.

Then there was the rabbit that thought he was a guard dog, and gave thieves who broke into a pet shop at Didcot in Oxfordshire rather more than they'd bargained for. He looked harmless enough, but deep down inside he hated men and liked to get his teeth into them. He was locked up during the day and only released at night to keep an eye on the place. The burglars retreated empty-handed. His owner says women are safe – but he's put a man in hospital.

One of the things about newscasting is that you can't afford to get a frog in your throat – or, for that matter, a moth. An Australian newscaster was in the middle of an important news bulletin when a moth flew straight into his mouth. In desperation he swallowed it – and read on. The next day the Australian Broadcasting Commission promoted him. If you want to get ahead, get a moth.

An internal disorder of a different kind drew a vet to a farm in Holland. A cow's stomach had become swollen with gas. The vet put a tube into the cow, and lit a match to test the escaping gas. There was an explosion followed by a fire which set light to bales of hay and burned the farm to the ground. The vet and the cow were shocked but unharmed.

Twelve-year-old James Showers from Wangford in East Sussex hatched the egg of a wild duck by keeping it in his armpit for three weeks. He said he found the egg abandoned in a hedge during the holidays – and it eventually hatched during dinner-time at his boarding school near Oxford. Too late to change the menu, though.

The British Hedgehog Preservation Society (yes, it really does exist!) came up with what they hoped was a real lifesaver for the little spiky creatures. The hedgehog's biggest enemy, it seems, is not another wild animal – but the farmer's cattle grid. Thousands of them fall down between the iron bars and can't get out. Many die of starvation. So the Society raised thousands of pounds to build tiny ramps that will provide the little wanderers with escape routes out of every cattle grid. Another prickly problem solved!

And just in case animals find coping with the strain of modern life just too much to bear, Taronga Park Zoo in Australia has come up with the answer – tranquillizer drugs administered to the animals with their food. Sir Edward Hallstrom, Chairman of the Zoo, said the drugs had cured many zoo inmates of "emotional stress and anti-social behaviour".

At Kansas City Zoo, vets put the spring back into the stride of a crippled kangaroo. A bad infection left the vets with no choice but to amputate the unfortunate animal's foot. They toyed with the idea of making an artificial foot – until someone came up with a better idea. They fitted him with a Size 13 child's sneaker. Now they say he's improving by leaps and bounds.

Roll up Hetty the Tortoise – game for anything now that toy wheels help her to get around. Hetty injured a back leg, and her shell

was so heavy the leg didn't have a chance to recover. The vet recommended some wheels – and Hetty, who obviously wished to be ready to tackle a hare at any time, agreed. The Baker family, who keep her in training around Shepherd's Bush, say Hetty is much better than they thought going uphill. Parking may be a problem, but she still shows other tortoises a clean pair of wheels.

Surgeons in America have turned turtle by carrying out the world's first *flipper* transplant. Lucky, as the turtle was inevitably called, lost her front flippers in a shark attack while she was swimming with her mate off the Florida Keys. Television pictures of her plight touched the hearts of millions of Americans. So the Goodyear Tyre Company and a team of medical experts designed artificial rubber flippers, which were grafted on in a three-hour operation. The total cost – over $200,000. Her next step? Rejoining her mate in the sea.

Critics in New York decided that an American composer had really gone to the dogs. His latest work was a 35-minute sonata – for dogs. It was performed in public for the first time at Carnegie Hall – and just to help the dogs strike the right note the audience was encouraged to sing along too. As to how he'd trained the dogs to strike the right note, the composer kept that a closely guarded secret.

What's in a name? A very great deal if recent appointments to the Royal Society for the Protection of Birds were anything to go by. Their headquarters in Bedfordshire had among its staff a Mr Alan Bird, Barbara Buzzard, John Partridge, Celia and Helen Peacock, Dorothy Rook and Peter Condor (recently retired).

The full weight of officialdom swung into action when a soldier returned home from a NATO exercise in Denmark with an unusual companion – a mouse. The mouse was discovered in his suitcase, and it was immediately slung into quarantine for six months – just in case it was carrying rabies. Easy enough for it to go missing. Not so easy for an 800 lb baby elephant in Copenhagen Zoo. Yet thieves broke into the zoo and spirited the elephant away in what was clearly

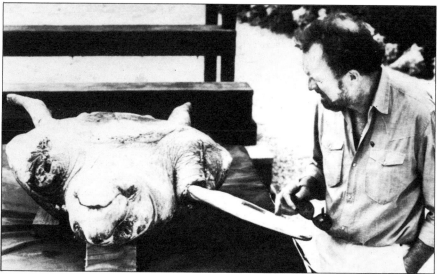

a carefully planned operation. It was snatched from under the trunks of two grown elephants, marched through the dark and deserted garden, taken out through a large hole cut in the fence and driven off in a truck or van. And, said police, they didn't leave behind a single clue.

One heavyweight that shows no sign of leaving home is Himmy, the fattest, heaviest cat in the world. Himmy weighs just over three stone, has a 30-inch waist and a 15-inch neck. Why he's so fat is a complete mystery. His Australian owner says he was a normal-sized kitten and doesn't overeat. People find Himmy a shade too large to pick up and cuddle – they show their affection by taking him for walks in a wheelbarrow.

And finally, American Bill Steed's affections lie in another direction. His mission is to train frogs to the peak of mental and physical fitness. So he hypnotizes them and plays what he calls a "character reinforcement recording" into their ears through tiny speakers. Then he puts them through a series of weight-lifting exercises with a set of specially made miniature weights. Then he tells them to hop off!

EXCUSES, EXCUSES

A driver who was fined £10 for speeding near Rochdale told the magistrate he'd had great difficulty in seeing what speed he was doing. He said: "I know it sounds incredible, but a few days before the offence a rather large spider crawled into the speedometer and span a web over the dial."

A 23-year-old Swede was driving a vanload of mice to a Gothenburg hospital for use in experiments when he skidded off the road. He told the court that the breath of hundreds of mice fogged the windscreen so badly that he had to bend down to pick up a cloth to wipe it clear – and that was when he landed up in the ditch. The court wasn't entirely convinced. He was fined 15 days' pay.

A Bolton entertainer Robin Robertson pleaded guilty to driving a motorcycle with more than the permitted level of alcohol in his blood. But the defending counsel explained that his client was a fire-eater by profession, whose secret was to "fill his mouth with methylated spirit so that the vapour emitted gives the illusion of fire coming out of his mouth, and some of the meths could sometimes trickle down his throat". The court decided that Mr Robertson had no reason to think the alcohol would not have affected him. He was fined – but not disqualified from driving.

Stornoway police on a routine patrol stopped to investigate noises coming from the back of a parked truck, and came across Donald MacAuley and a couple of friends. The three men were, the local court was told, "well oiled with drink". Upon being discovered, MacAuley – said the police – promptly swallowed the truck's ignition key. And to prove the allegation the police produced an X-ray of MacAuley's stomach. But that was one piece of evidence the sheriff refused to accept – on the grounds that the police had neglected to obtain a search warrant before they took the X-ray.

In Johannesburg, police and firemen were called to rescue a man who was stuck in a chimney. The house-owner thought it was a pigeon and lit some paper in the grate to try and smoke it out. The man in the chimney, when charged later with attempted burglary, told the court he'd lost his way while visiting a friend.

Another burglar nearly did himself in at a Do-It-Yourself shop
in Chesterfield. Getting into the shop was easy – but getting out
quickly when the alarm went off turned out to be a little more
difficult. In the dark, the man tried twelve doors without realizing
they were just there for display. Each time he opened one he ran into
a brick wall. It disturbed him so much that he fell down a staircase –
and knocked himself out. Police say he may have had a drink or two.

Two Glasgow thieves picked an unusual vehicle to make their getaway. One was seen pushing his accomplice with a television set away from the scene of the crime – in a wheelchair. Their lawyer told the court: "It's less conspicuous than a car."

When Edward Szuluk was remanded in Gloucester on a serious assault charge, he at least knew that his wife Wendy was sticking by him. She put super-glue on her hands – and rushed over to hold his. But though they were thus joined together, they were eventually put asunder – by hospital doctors.

A man on remand in Leeds prison was "released" rather more easily – in time for Christmas. Doncaster magistrates allowed bail after being told that the man's brother would keep him "under constant vigilance" in "the strictest security in the country". The brother turned out to be a caretaker in the Tower of London.

A Bristol man was fined £20 for impersonating his father-in-law. The father-in-law had failed his driving test four times, and so the son-in-law, who was a qualified driver, offered to take it for him. The examiner failed him too.

Not a good day either for a man who tried to hold up a shop in Michigan in America. He dropped his gun twice, shot at a customer and missed, had to push his getaway car to a filling station because he'd run out of gas, and was refused service because it was past closing time. Then he was arrested.

In Tokyo, a man accused of a hundred and eight offences told the court that seventy-one of them had been trumped up by policemen who wanted to win a national contest for the biggest number of successful prosecutions. The man said he'd been treated to rice, wine and free cinema seats for confessing to the crimes. He was acquitted. The policemen were arrested.

Two American policewomen were sacked by the police department in Detroit – for cowardice. Their offence was failing to go to the aid of a male police officer who was being attacked. The attacker, from whom the lady officers flinched, was a naked man burning money in the street.

From Australia – the story of the man who went duck-shooting on a Sunday. He was bitten on the arm by a snake – so to save his life he deliberately shot himself in the arm to bleed the poison out. It worked – and he quickly recovered in hospital – but that wasn't the end of his troubles. The local court fined him one pound for carrying a firearm on a Sunday.

And finally, Rolls Royce in Bristol fired an 18-year-old apprentice because, they said, his hair was dangerous and could have injured other workers. Peter Mortiboy, who was a punk and made his hair stand on end using super-glue, appealed against his dismissal – but lost. He also wore 18 earrings and had to be given a special place to sit during exams because the noise of them all jangling together distracted the other apprentices. Obviously a very sharp young man.

TIME ON THEIR HANDS

"Take a letter" has a whole new meaning for Mrs Gwen James, who worked in the china department of a big Wolverhampton store. She was sent a letter via the store's internal postal system, addressed to G.D. James, 36312 – which was her staff number. The letter slipped into the external mail by mistake, and finally reached Mrs James a full two months later – having been to Peking and back.

WELCOME BACK GWENS LETTER TWO MONTHS LATE!

STAFF CANTE

'... DUE TO YOUR CONTINUED LACK OF PUNCTUALITY YOUR SERVICES ARE NO LONGER REQUIRED...'

Back, in 1933, a woman living in Donegal posted a piece of wedding cake to her brother, who lived just under a mile away. The parcel, addressed to Maghery, went to Australia, North and South America and right through Asia, as one post office after another tried desperately to get it right. The cake finally arrived at its destination 30 years later.

Even so, that was good going compared with the Christmas card posted in Canada in 1911, which finally arrived at its destination in New Jersey, USA, 57 years later. And they say post early for Christmas!

Time doesn't seem to have been on the side of Luigi Gandolfo, an Italian soldier wounded in the finger during the First World War. In 1925 he applied to what was then the Ministry of War for a pension. They finally got round to giving him one 56 years later. But it was hardly worth waiting for – a mere 2p a month for three years.

Birmingham Council were rather more charitable when they discovered an employee who hadn't had a pay rise for 28 years. She was a 57-year-old charlady who'd soldiered on without a word of complaint on exactly the same wages they'd been paying her when she joined the staff in 1948. The council did the decent thing. They wrote her a cheque for £4,000 back-pay on the spot, and told her there'd be more on the way once they'd done all their sums.

A gendarme at St Quentin in France never quite forgot the embarrassing day in 1940 when someone stole his bicycle. He finally tracked it down in a nearby village – 27 years later. An elderly man is helping with inquiries.

It wasn't detective work but Mother Nature that helped to recover a crate of books lost overboard in the Pacific Ocean in 1945. They belonged to a former prisoner of the Japanese forces returning to his home town of Wigan. Exactly 20 years later the books were washed up on the Lancashire coast just 25 miles from his home. And they were in good condition!

Time literally stood still for one Japanese soldier who spent 31

years hiding in the Indonesian jungle because he didn't know the Second World War was over. When he finally got home he found his wife had got tired of waiting and remarried. But she was so pleased to see him she decided to get a divorce and marry him all over again. As

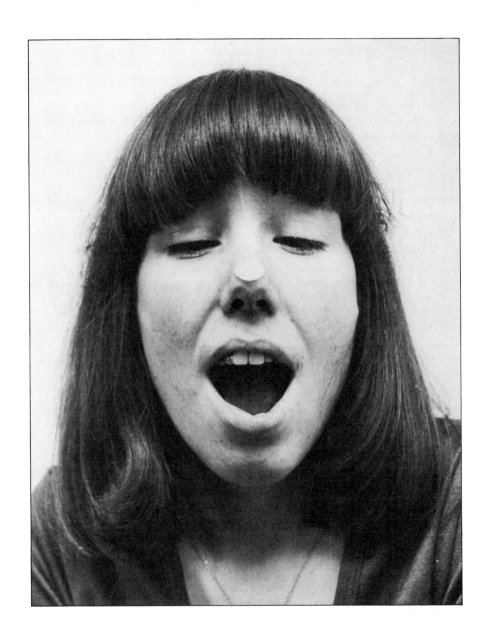

compensation the second husband got $2,500 – and a water buffalo. Honour – if not the second husband – was satisfied.

Another married couple were reunited in Blackpool after 34 years apart. They'd separated when the husband returned to England soon after they'd emigrated to America. He promised that as soon as he'd saved enough money, he'd send her the fare so she could join him. But somehow he never got round to it. So she eventually sold their house in Detroit to pay for the passage herself. They were both in their seventies when they got together again – with a lot of catching up to do.

Suffolk hospital porter George Niles and his wife felt the urge to get together rather more quickly. She went to Barbados to look after her sick parents, and after she'd been there a year George decided to cheer her up by paying a surprise visit. But no sooner had he left on the 3,000-mile journey when his wife, who'd had exactly the same idea, arrived unexpectedly in Suffolk. After a little help from the Barbados government, they finally got their act – and themselves – together in Barbados.

And finally, the story of the lady who was at last able to breathe easy. Ruth Clark had had sinus trouble for 20 years – ever since she was a three-year-old baby. Her doctor tried everything, but eventually gave up and called in a surgeon. He found the cause of the trouble – a half-inch tiddlywink stuck up her left nostril.

LOVE AND MARRIAGE

Two Italian gourmets, in love with the same woman, agreed to have an eating duel to decide who should marry her. After they'd each waded through three plates of spaghetti, one roast duck, twenty sausages, ten eggs in sauce, half a large cream cake and sixteen steaks, one of them finally dropped out. The winner, Nicola Di Attista, went on to polish off another steak. But it was all in vain. The woman, a pretty young school teacher, said she was so disgusted by their greed that she wouldn't marry either of them.

Mike Rowley, from Patchway near Bristol, discovered another obstacle to marriage. The day before his wedding, friends took him out to celebrate, locked him into a chastity belt, and threw the key into the river. The local fire brigade freed him with a hacksaw and none-too-straight faces all round. The future Mrs Rowley was *not* amused.

At least she didn't have to put off the wedding – which is more than you can say for Miss Agatha Kenchington from Jersey, whose childhood sweetheart, François Aufret, finally named the day after a 29-year engagement. He was 64. She was 72. After the ceremony a happy Agatha said: "It's a big step, but I'm sure we'll never regret it."

That would hardly impress Californian Nina Duden whose engagement lasted all of 44 years. She was 68, and he a sprightly 72, when they finally made it to the altar. Looking at the engagement ring, given to her before the First World War, Nina said: "This is its fourth setting and the band of gold's nearly worn through again."

Some people don't believe in engagements at all. Others don't even get the chance of one. Peter Graddon turned up at a Plymouth Registrar's Office after his girlfriend asked him to witness a friend renewing her marriage vows. But the girlfriend arrived in a bride's outfit, popped the question – and Peter ended up as a bridegroom.

There isn't much that millionaire playboy Tommy Manville couldn't tell you about engagements and marriages. By the time he was 63 he'd been married ten times. His tenth bride – Pat Gatson, a striking blonde chorus girl from a New York show – insisted she wasn't marrying him for his money because "after nine alimonies he couldn't have much left". Miss Gatson's mother, asked to comment on her new son-in-law's previous marriages, said: "I feel that he's been searching for something."

So, it seems, was a 28-year-old man from Northern Sumatra, who, under Muslim law, was allowed up to four wives at any one time. He actually married a total of 128 – but only got round to divorcing 93 of them. So the father of one of his last brides had a charge of polygamy brought against him, claiming in passing that his daughter had been fed "only on bananas". The husband went to jail for seven years.

Some ladies aren't too keen to let their husbands go – even if it is only for a stag night with some friends. In the Italian town of Latina it led to quite a row for one couple.

She wanted him to stay at home. *He* insisted on leaving. *She* grabbed the key to the front door and swallowed it. *He* had to break the door down to get her to hospital to have the key removed. *And* he didn't get his night out with the boys.

Sometimes it's better not to know what the other half is doing. A Yorkshireman was fined in court for not declaring his wife's earnings to the tax collector. It seemed that she was working in nightclubs as "Baby Doll", the topless fire-eater. *He* thought she was visiting her mother.

Deception of a different kind in Indiana. A man asked a judge to annul his marriage after just six weeks on the grounds that his wife – who'd been married before – had been guilty of fraud. She'd told him she had three children. He later found out she had ten. He told the court: "She just keeps bringing more and more children into the house."

A 23-year-old American model was granted a divorce from a businessman she'd married 18 months earlier. She said he'd told her he was 57. After they were married she discovered he was really 91.

Even after divorce, the battle isn't always over. A Seattle woman was awarded increased alimony payments after she described her ex-husband's lifestyle to the judge. She said the master bedroom had a small, but deep, bathing pool in one corner, while in another corner was a trout pool fed by a natural stream. And the adjoining bathroom had wine and beer on tap.

And finally, it's a sad fact that the happiest of marriages can run into problems. After 17 years of wedded bliss, a French restaurateur was told that a clerical error had led to his father's name being entered on his marriage certificate instead of his own. So – until a court of law put matters right – his father was officially a bigamist, he was a bachelor, his sons were his half-brothers and his wife was his stepmother.

SHAKEN AND STIRRED

Some official backing for those who need alcohol in their bloodstream came from Professor C.G. Rob of London University. He told a British Medical Association conference: "The best drug for the relief of pain is alcohol – and I don't mean anything pharmaceutical. I mean whisky!"

That could be catching! A Ministry of Health Appeal Board ruled that gin *can* be prescribed on the National Health under certain circumstances. A Middlesex doctor had prescribed a mixture of morphine, cocaine and gin, but the local executive council said they were not bound to supply the gin. The Appeal Board said they were. Fancy popping along to the doctor's surgery for a quick snort?

Most drinkers would tell you that "The White Horse" is either the name of a pub or a whisky. Grimsby magistrates heard another version as a police constable described the scene of his latest arrest. "Last night," he said, "I saw a white horse standing in the square at Laceby (a village near Grimsby). Round its neck was a halter with a long rope attached. At the other end of this rope was a man leaning against the bar of the Nag's Head Inn. I saw the man step out of the pub, get under the horse and try to lift it, saying as he did so: "This is Taffy – I love her more than my wife." The outcome of the case? The man was fined for being drunk in charge of a horse.

After an unsuccessful day at Stornoway market, farmer Malcolm MacIver drowned his sorrows in the local pub – and then started walking home along with the cow he'd failed to sell. But cows are unpredictable creatures at the best of times – and the paths of both man and beast were erratic to say the least. The local policeman decided to intervene, but the cow was having none of that. It bolted – dragging the law into disrepute, and through the mud as well. MacIver proved a little easier to stop. He was arrested and fined £15 by the local sheriff. The charge? Drunk in charge of a cow.

It wouldn't surprise the inhabitants of Sacramento in California. Their local council approved a law allowing the charge of drunken or reckless driving to be brought against people on roller skates and in wheelchairs.

Whichever way heavy drinkers choose to go home, it seems the law will catch up with them. So perhaps the answer is not to go home at all. A tramp once got locked in the Portsmouth branch of Woolworths on Christmas Eve – and when staff opened up four days later they found he'd had a merry, if lonely, time. Police had to wait another day before he'd sobered up and they could identify him. Here was one man who needed no persuading about the "Wonder of Woolworths".

The wonder of the Arts Council's grants system came in for some criticism in the House of Commons. It seems they'd given a grant to three students who walked around East Anglia with a yellow plank on their heads. An MP said that this so-called "mobile sculpture" had been observed calling in at a fair number of pubs. The Education Ministry said it was up to the Arts Council to choose how it spent its money.

In the French town of Metz the drinkers must have thought their eternal nightmare was coming true when a man walked into a bar with an elephant in tow. But they needn't have worried – or had cause to pinch themselves. It was merely one of the locals, who was so angry that dogs were allowed into his favourite watering hole that he decided to test the owner's claim that *all* animals were admitted. So he borrowed Chita, who weighed a ton, from a nearby zoo. To his surprise, Chita was welcomed just like anyone else, and served his favourite drink – orange juice – in a two-litre ice bucket. But it was an expensive round – it cost five pounds. The barman said he wasn't changing the rules – and Chita was welcome back any time!

Australian Bill Foster claims he can down a beer before you can say "Cheers". Well, almost every pub has got someone who says they can do that. The difference is that Bill does it standing on his head. It's no trick, either. He just utters the magic words "Ziggy, zoggy, ziggy, zoggy" and a pint of beer defies the law of gravity and makes its way rapidly to his stomach suspended eighteen inches *above* his mouth. Bill's become quite a tourist attraction – and, not surprisingly, is a welcome visitor in any pub.

A bar in Southern Oregon has hit on a way of serving cocktails that makes sure that those in search of a stiff drink end up with a stiff neck as well. The drinkers lie back in a barber's chair – and the barmaid mixes the drink in the mouth. No-one's quite sure what happens if you order a double, but it's best to get your cocktails stirred not shaken.

Some drink is strictly for the birds. A man who catches pigeons on public buildings by first getting them drunk has been warned he may be breaking the law which protects birds. But John Cameron,

who's already put his method to good use in several towns, says his method of doping the pigeons with grain soaked in whisky is a very humane way of getting rid of them. It's also economical. According to Mr Cameron, one bottle of whisky will dispose of about a thousand birds.

And one bottle of vodka disposed of one Mr Popov, a Soviet Communist Party official. He was out picnicking with some comrades when they were accidentally sprayed with fertilizer by a low-flying plane. Mr Popov was so incensed he hurled a bottle of vodka at the offending aircraft, and scored a direct hit. The plane was forced to crash-land in a nearby field. There were no happy landings for Mr Popov either. He was sacked from his job and expelled from the party. And the Soviet government newspaper *Izvestia* published the sad story as a warning to fellow citizens not to abuse their national drink.

And finally, Japanese farmers have produced a new liqueur. It has, they say, a "delicate, apple-like flavour" – which helps to conceal the fact that it's made out of dead earthworms. But the Japanese, never at a loss for a good marketing ploy, insist that it puts more zest into your love life. They're clearly out to improve productivity in every possible way!

WE WILL WITHDRAW ALL CRUISE MISSILES
IF THE USSR AGREES TO REMOVE ALL
OF ITS VODKA BOTTLES...

GOOD SPORTS

You've got to be very young indeed not to remember the days when soccer players fell all over each other when their side scored a goal. If it doesn't happen quite so often now, you can thank the International Football Federation, FIFA, who told the lads quite bluntly that "the kissing and hugging" had to stop. FIFA felt it was "unmanly and provocative", and "the exultant outburst of players

POOR DEVIL. HE'LL JUST HAVE TO BE SATISFIED WITH A FIFA KISSOGRAM!

jumping on top of each other, and kissing and embracing each other, was excessive, inappropriate and should be banned".

Which makes you wonder what they thought of Coventry City, who were sixth in the First Division when they decided to send their star players to ballet school. The coach decided that graceful exercises to the "Dance of the Sugar Plum Fairy" might improve their coordination. The team, who were more used to passes than pas-de-deux, and preferred late kick-offs to leotards, appeared to take it stoically enough. The fans, however, made it pretty clear what they thought about it all on the terraces the following Saturday.

While Coventry thought they had found a remedy that might help them win, Bristol Rovers were absolutely certain why *they* were losing. They blamed Police Superintendent Vince Arkell, the man in charge of police at home games. It didn't matter that he was a keen supporter – or that his father used to play for the side. The fact was that the only time Bristol Rovers had won that season, Superintendent Arkell hadn't been there. So the club decided he was a bit of a jinx – and promptly banned him for the rest of the season. Even then, they weren't entirely certain they'd done the right thing. The very next match – against Notts County – ended in a one-all draw.

An Italian Fourth Division side – also losing regularly in home matches – decided on an even more drastic remedy. The Borgosesia manager called in the parish priest to exorcize the pitch after fans complained that only ghosts could have caused the town to lose five games in a row. I suppose no-one thought of blaming the players.

One man who did was the referee in one of England's more ruthless soccer tournaments. The crack team from the Cheshire Police League in Runcorn were lined up against the champions of the Ellesmere Port Sub-Division. At stake was no less a prize than the Chief Constable's Cup. Alas for the guardians of law and order, the referee abandoned the game at half-time, because, he said, "it had been forty minutes of aggravated assault". He later explained: "Police football has never been soft, but I was concerned for the safety of the players." No doubt much of what they said was taken down in writing and could be used in evidence.

At least they didn't suffer the fate of the Irish League soccer team Glenavon. After they'd been soundly thrashed five-nil, their manager announced he was putting *all* the players on the transfer list. But he hastily added that it wasn't because of their performance – it was just that they wanted too much money.

Not every soccer player with a bad track record gets shown the door. Regulars at the Wharncliffe Hotel in Barnsley voted their goalkeeper "Player of the Year" despite the fact that he let through 120 goals during the season. "Without him," they said, "it would have been much worse. He's the best player on the side."

No prizes, though, for Duke the Alsatian guard dog, recruited to keep night-time vandals away from the South Pacific Tennis Tournament in Australia. Unbeknown to the organizers, Duke suffered from night starvation. In the morning they found he'd left his post, and dug up part of the Centre Court looking for bones.

Golf has certainly slowed up considerably at Tuam Golf Club near Galway in the West of Ireland. Players have reported losing a lot of balls – not because of the rough, but because of a large crow. It's carried off dozens of members' balls – on one occasion more than twenty in one day – by snatching them off the course and dropping them out of bounds, and out of reach, in a nearby bog. Among its victims were two golfers on a short hole who'd both made the green in one, and could only watch in fury as the bird swooped down and carried off both balls.

Then there was the day that golfer Michael Bonallack, playing in the Amateur Golf championship at Formby in Lancashire, reached the fourth round by a nose – a spectator's nose. At the 14th hole his bunker shot struck the unfortunate observer on the nose, and bounced onto the green instead of ploughing into a nasty piece of rough. As a result Bonnallack halved the hole. He continued to nose ahead – and eventually won by four and three.

Another shot that some fans didn't appreciate occurred during a cricket match between the West Indies and New South Wales in Sydney. Batsman Desmond Haynes struck a magnificent six. The ball flew right out of the ground and into a ladies' lavatory. Play was delayed for several minutes while a woman spectator went in to retrieve it. One commentator made a joke about "fielding in the slips", and Haynes went on to score 139 – no doubt flushed with his own success.

In a club match in Australia a fast bowler delivered what can only be described as a real scorcher. The batsman's trousers burst into flames when the ball hit him on the thigh. It seems he'd left a box of matches in his pocket.

Another cricketer who was too hot to handle ended up getting divorced by his wife. She said that cricket had always been his first love and she couldn't compete with it. Mrs Mildred Rowley told the court that the game had become a "total obsession" with her husband, who'd been Stourbridge's official scorer for 21 years. He could, she said, remember cricket statistics from years ago – but not her birthday. Her husband didn't turn up in court – he was touring with the club. But he did say: "I don't blame Mildred. Cricket's the only life for me."

You never know when cricketing skills are going to come in handy. Former cricketer Lawrence Houson made the catch of his life when a neighbour's two-year-old son fell 35 feet from a window. Mr Houson moved quickly enough to knock little Stephen Bamforth away from some iron railings, and then caught him by the ankle before he hit the ground. He modestly put his life-saving catch down to his early experience on the cricket pitch.

And finally, there was no-one around to catch French stuntman Philippe Petit when, with the help of a bow and arrow, he slung a tightrope between the twin towers of the world's tallest inhabited building – the World Trade Centre in New York. Crowds gathered on the pavement 1,300 feet below as Philippe crossed the 90-foot gap several times. Eventually the police arrived – and took him

away to be examined by a psychiatrist. He said: "When I see three oranges, I have to juggle. When I see two towers, I have to walk."

NAUGHTY BUT NICE

For those too young to remember, "The Twist" was a dance that turned into a craze during the 1960s. So much so that the fashion magazine *Tailor and Cutter* was moved to offer advice on topless twisting: "The dangers engendered through dancing with a bare-bosomed lady are, after all, slight. There would be no impropriety at all in the close-locked stance of a night-club shuffle; and even in the wilder gyrations of a twist or a jig the worst damage one could suffer would be a well-bruised carnation."

Travelling fan dancer Sally Rand didn't get a chance to do much bruising at a night club in Omaha, Nebraska, before the local police started throwing *their* weight around. Sally had only been through her routine once when she was arrested. The police said her act "went beyond the bounds of propriety". Sally's defence was that she'd been giving the same performance for 32 years without any trouble. She gave her age as 61.

There was bad luck of another kind for an Arab who came to London and had a fertility operation. He'd hardly been released from hospital before he was arrested and fined £10 for pinching a lady's bottom. Obviously another triumph for British medicine.

The United States Army went so far as to bring charges of sexual harassment against a woman. It happened at Nuremberg in West Germany, where GI Cheryl Taylor of Kansas City was accused of grabbing GI Kevin Knox in the dispensary, manhandling him, calling him a shrimp and demanding a light. He objected to her unsolicited advances and complained to a senior officer. In court, the prosecutor said the Army was getting a poorer-quality soldier today. GI Cheryl Taylor was sentenced to 30 days' hard labour, fined $298 and demoted. On hearing her sentence Miss Taylor said she'd joined the Army to avoid men.

And finally, naked aggression showed it did have a softer face

£10, AND WE'LL CHUCK IN A FERTILITY OPERATION AS WELL!

in West Berlin. About fifty demonstrators attending an international squatters' festival took off their clothes to show the peaceful nature of their protest. The message got through – the police, appropriately enough, turned the other cheek.

DIFFICULT DELIVERIES

An expectant mother was being rushed to hospital in the Israeli town of Beersheba when the car she was travelling in collided with a stork. One hour later the mother gave birth to a healthy, bouncing boy. The stork was stunned and slightly injured, and was rushed to the local vet. Mother and baby are doing fine. Latest reports say the stork is as well as can be expected.

Some storks put in quite a bit of overtime. In America three sisters gave birth to three baby boys in the same hospital on the same day. It's not easy to top that – but a 42-year-old Nottingham man had a pretty good try. He became a father *and* a grandfather on the same day. His second wife had a son in Nottingham City hospital – and three hours later his 21-year-old daughter from his first marriage also had a son.

Then there's the business of choosing the baby's name. Plenty of couples have arguments over that – but few go as far as the George family from Cardiff. Mrs Lynette George actually left her husband Trevor because she didn't like the names he put on their daughter's birth certificate. Trevor, who was – to put it mildly – a football fanatic, had named her after 20 world soccer stars – Jennifer Pele Jairzinho Rivelino Alberto Cesar Breitner Cruyff Greaves Charlton Best Moore Ball Keegan Banks Gray Francis Brooking Curtis Toshack Law George! Mrs George decided she had to blow the whistle on that, and walked out. But a month later the family were a united team again, after Mrs George had been to Cardiff Register Office to rename the baby Jennifer Anne. Both mum and dad have agreed that those will be the names on any future fixture lists.

We all know that babies are notorious for getting into trouble. But they don't often end up in a court of law. That's what happened to 18-month-old Maurizio Pesca from Turin, who was fined 400 lira for continually sounding the horn of the family car after his father had parked it to go shopping. Dad did the decent thing – and paid up

with a grin.

Eighteen months is fast becoming a key age for youngsters who want to make an early mark in life. One boy in Birmingham picked up a handful of darts when his father's back was turned, and amazed everyone by throwing them at the board and scoring 180.

Another 18-month-old set to make a big splash is Parkes Bonifay from Florida. His parents are professional waterskiers, and it was only a matter of time before he asked if baby could come too. So a special set of skis was built, Parkes hopped on, and off went the speedboat at a mere five miles an hour with Dad at the controls. Despite the inevitable duckings, Parkes really looked as if he was enjoying it. And if he's found with a wet nappy, at least he's got a good excuse.

What would you do if you saw your 18-month-old daughter walking across the garden clutching a poisonous black snake? That's what happened to Mr and Mrs Stiles in Melbourne, Australia, and not surprisingly they rushed towards her in a panic. But they needn't have worried. Baby Diana wasn't just holding the snake, she was chewing it. And by the time her parents reached her she'd bitten the snake's head off, without being bitten herself. By way of explanation her father said Diana was teething. "She'd bite through your finger if you gave her the chance," he said.

In South Africa a 16-foot python met its match when it attacked a 14-year-old black herd boy. The boy thumped it with a stick – and then sank his teeth into the python's neck. The python never recovered – and it took two men to carry its body away, proving once again that snakes ought to attack people their own size.

And finally, if keeping an eye on children all becomes too much for you, then a St Albans man could have the answer. He's built a talking computer that's programmed to react to his daughter's voice, and answer back soothingly in either his voice or his wife's. But does it ever lose its temper?

HOUSE CALL

Perfect landlords aren't easy to find. But 86-year-old James Bricker from Harrisburg in Pennsylvania has to be a top candidate for the title. A property man in a small way, he earned a comfortable income by renting out nine three-bedroomed houses which he owned. One day he decided that over the years the tenants had more than paid the cost of the houses in rent, so he offered them a chance to buy them. Before anyone could start arguing over just how much they were worth, Mr Bricker named his asking price – a mere $10 apiece. (In those days that worked out at about £3.75.)

A wooden house, built in the 1870s and in fine condition on a prime riverside site, was sold for a more realistic, indeed substantial, price to a Florida businessman. The snag was he wanted the land it was built on, and not the building itself. Not wishing to be regarded as a vandal destroying part of his country's history he advertised the house for sale *without* the land beneath it. The house was levered onto a barge on the river – caught someone's eye – a deal was done – and a genuine piece of Americana floated off to a new site downstream. But then, moving house always was a tricky business.

And sometimes it happens by accident. Italian Antonio Bisogna didn't know his own strength. When a window in his flat got stuck, he hammered on the shutters so hard that the wall fell down. Antonio fled into the street, followed by five families who lived in the same apartment block. They were just in time. The entire three-storey building collapsed behind them.

Three hundred and fifty singers from Women's Institutes in Essex had another lucky escape – at a music festival in Chelmsford. "Sing as you've never sung before," they were told. "Raise the roof if you like." They did – and part of it fell in. The contralto section caught the full force of the fall – four of them had to be treated for cuts in hospital. They said the real reason for the collapse was vibration

set up by workmen on another part of the roof. But we know better!

And finally, there's the kind of house-move that no-one is expecting. A Scottish court actually found a man guilty of *stealing* a house. Witnesses said that the man and some others unknown arrived in a lorry and removed a prefabricated house from a building site. He was ordered to be detained in the most secure accommodation in the land for six months!

CONTINUING EMBARRASSMENT

The thing about tailpieces is that just when you think you've heard them all, yet another bizarre combination of circumstances bounces in to surprise you – an old story with a new twist, or, more usually, some tale that no fiction writer would dare to include for fear it would threaten his credibility. All the more remarkable that such stories have cropped up with astounding regularity over the three decades that ITN has been hunting them. And still they come in! As proof, here are some offerings from the last few months.

A special ceremony in London rewarded two men whose enthusiasm and dedication to their work made a tiny – but important – part of many people's lives a great deal more comfortable. Les Harding and his partner Reg received the Golden Loo Award for the best-kept public lavatory in Britain. The carefully inscribed mahogany toilet seat was handed over to the two lavatory attendants who used their own money to make sure others could "spend a penny" in comfort. Jim Reeves singing *Welcome to my World* in stereo welcomes customers to an establishment where the usual graffiti have been replaced by flowers and pictures, and there's an abundance of fresh soap, clean towels and even nailbrushes. Flushed with their new-found success, Reg and Les explained they were proud of their loo, they did it "for the public", and their aim was to offer "value for money". And where do you find this exceptional emporium? Where else but in London WC2!

In Oxfordshire, equal dedication by two ladies – but instead of a reward, a rebuke. Molly and Flora had worked hard at cultivating their garden, quietly and inoffensively. Until the green-fingered duo moved in, it had been a wild, unkempt piece of land. They planted flowers, watered it, weeded it, and generally won the admiration of most passers-by. But then the local council ordered them to stop. You see, Molly and Flora's adopted garden was a traffic roundabout in

the middle of a road junction outside their home! It didn't matter that the beautifying of the roundabout didn't cost the ratepayers a penny. Rules were rules – and freelance operators weren't allowed on roundabouts!

But they do all right in New York. Where else – outside Asia – would you find *two*-wheeled taxis? Paul Irgang, a keen cyclist, already knew that pedal power was the best way to beat the rush-hour traffic jams in Manhattan. So he bought a fleet of tandems, hired a few friends who were tall in the saddle, and put out the Yellow Cab sign. Business boomed. It was quite surprising how many New Yorkers had a hankering to ride pillion – even if they did have to do some of the work. Not much chance to read a paper or start one of those legendary New York conversations with the driver, but at ten cents a block Paul reckons he's put a spoke in the cab drivers' wheels.

Terence Talbot wished he'd taken a taxi – however many wheels it had. He was due in court and decided to drive himself there. But Terence had a car crash en route, so he set off to walk the rest of the way . . . and got run over. When he didn't turn up in court, the judge ordered his arrest. He eventually got bail, and a friend reminded him of the date – Friday the 13th.

When Mrs Janet Hill dropped in on her local bank she did so in considerable style. She landed her Ford Escort car on the roof of Lloyds Bank at Dawlish in Devon – after crashing through the safety barrier of a multi-storey car park next door. Mrs Hill was unhurt, but her car was a write-off – one deposit that could only be withdrawn with the help of a crane.

You just can't bank on what a car is going to do next! A woman of 91 found out that life in the fast lane wasn't quite what it used to be when she started driving. Magistrates in West Sussex disqualified her for going too slowly – 15 mph on a road where the speed limit was 60 mph. They congratulated her on her clean driving licence – seventy years without a blemish – then invited her to take the driving test that hadn't been necessary when she first hit the road.

Sir Sandy Woodward passed the test all right – he commanded the British Naval Task Force that helped rescue the Falkland islanders from the Argentine invasion. But later, in quieter waters off the Hampshire coast, he had to be rescued himself when his 22-foot yacht lost its mast and he ended up being towed into port by a passing minesweeper.

The Falklands conflict also provided one of ITN's happiest tailpieces – the end of a story that began in tragedy. A Falklands farmer, Tim Miller, was accidentally blinded in one eye by an RAF bomb. While he was recovering on the hospital ship *Uganda*, a Manchester girl called Elaine became his penpal. Four months later the couple were married – and who do you think was best man? Flight Lieutenant Mark Hare – the pilot who dropped that bomb! Tim and Elaine said they were determined to show how much they appreciated the way in which they had been brought together.

Strange indeed are the paths that take some couples to the altar. Bruce and Sharon Leone met while jogging in the Seattle Marathon. It then seemed only right that they should run away to get married. So they tied the knot while taking part in the *next* Seattle Marathon. Their only problem was finding a minister prepared to

run backwards in front of them while they recited their vows. They eventually found one who was also the local church soccer coach. Kissing the bride proved to be a hit-and-miss affair.

An American fireman, Ralph Deal, loved his job so much he chose to get married inside a burning building during a fire department training exercise. Cheryl – the old flame that he married – looked glowing in a fireproof uniform. A fiery preacher led them through their vows, the TV crews turned up in force (positively fired with enthusiasm), and after the blaze of publicity they all went off to a cool reception. That was one wedding that really brought the house down!

Passport controllers at London's Heathrow Aiport got quite a shock when a man turned up claiming to be 160 years old. And in case there were any doubts, his official Pakistani passport gave his date of birth as 13 December 1823. Sayed Abdul Mabood has over 200 grandchildren, great grandchildren and great great grandchildren. He said he was flying TWA to Chicago "for minor hospital treatment". The man from the airline was doubtful about his age – he said Mr Mabood didn't look a day over 140.

You don't have to be very old these days to qualify for a facelift. Chester was only three years old when surgeons wheeled him in for his. But then, Chester was a particularly ugly *bulldog,* with more wrinkles than a dog four times his age. However, it wasn't his owner's vanity that prompted the operation – vets decided the huge wrinkles were a danger to his health. The operation was a success, and Chester is back to being just plain ugly!

It seems that dogs get more human every day. There's a mongrel called Rex who goes all goggle-eyed when his master gets out his motorbike – and he insists on going along too. Riding pillion isn't good enough for Rex. He insists on being up front, if only so the mere human driving the bike can stop him being blown off when the bike hits sixty miles an hour!

And if after that Rex needs a little relaxation, where better than a health farm in Tokyo that is strictly for dogs. The animals are put through a series of exercises carefully designed to ease the tensions of a dog's life. Surrounded by soothing music, they're pampered beyond their wildest dreams. What they're like to live with when they get back to reality, goodness knows.

One of the latest fitness crazes in California is a gym for babies. The theory is that you're never too young to join the world of sit-ups, knee-bends and arm-stretches. The instructors claim that playtime needs "extra stimulation" because the natural playgrounds of green grass and trees are rapidly being replaced with car parks. They also say the exercise classes "give the toddlers a new perspective on learning and fulfil a need for parents and children to get together".

A 13-year-old Greek boy, described as "the piano prodigy of the century", took London's Barbican Centre by storm when he went on stage with the London Symphony Orchestra. Dimitris Sgouros started playing at the age of six, became a Professor of Music when he was ten, and can now play 35 concertos from memory.

A 14-year-old South African schoolboy channelled his energy in a different direction when his brother needed a crucial eye operation. To help raise the money needed, Davie Victor set out to jump over nine cars – not on a motorbike, but on an ordinary bicycle. Speed, strong legs and sheer guts helped him do it. He soared into the air at 45 miles an hour, and – to everyone's relief – touched down for a perfect two-point landing.

New York pizza parlour waitress Phyllis Penza took rather longer to come down to earth after a customer made a most unusual offer. Police Sergeant Bob Cunningham offered her a share in a lottery ticket instead of his usual one-dollar tip. Phyllis accepted, and helped him pick the numbers. Between them they won the equivalent of four and a quarter million pounds.

Another handsome windfall came the way of a Glasgow couple who, on a visit to the Burrell Art Gallery, stopped in amazement in front of a 600-year-old Ming water jug. It was almost identical to the

copper-coloured container they used as a lamp in their drawing room at home. They sent it to an auction where it fetched £400,000 – not bad for an old lamp an uncle bought for £40.

Lady Luck can come to call in other ways. A 12-year-old yellow Labrador called Voss has run away with the title of the world's greatest canine lover. Voss is the top breeder for "Guide Dogs for the Blind", having fathered a record-breaking 567 puppies in ten years. Of this huge number, 460 have become guide dogs.

But Voss has a long way to go to catch up with an 11-year-old bull called Grove Speculator. The Milk Marketing Board, who own him, reckoned he was worth a double-page spread in their catalogue of super bulls. His achievement? So far he's fathered more than 220,000 calves to make him the undisputed world champion Dad. It's all done by artificial insemination, of course. But Grove Spectacular doesn't seem to mind. Veterinary officer Jackie Wallington described him as "one of the friendliest bulls we've got".

In America, the boffins are working to produce a new line of test-tube horses for show-jumping. And their first achievement is a young foal called Windrush E. Born in Tennessee, she's a cross between a top European sire and a thoroughbred American mare. At least 12 more of the breed – to be called "American Sporthorses" – are on the way.

Another American mare, from Kentucky, turned round to welcome her new-born foal and found she'd given birth to – a zebra. Vets said it was the first successful embryo transplant of its kind, and was a technique that could be used more widely to help endangered species.

Zebra crossings were really in fashion last year. A Northern Ireland zoo produced what they called a "Zonky" – part zebra, part donkey – which, they say, knocks spots, or rather stripes, off anything they've seen before. The foal was born at a safari park, and is one of the very few such crossbreeds to survive.

Mother Nature confounded the experts again at a wildlife park near Paris. First she produced an animal they called a "Ligron" – a cross between a lion and a tiger. Then the ligron herself gave birth to a cub. As animals roam the park quite freely, no-one's too sure who the father is – but it disproves claims that hybrid animals are sterile.

Mali, the St Bernard dog, gave everyone a lot to think about when she adopted a large litter of piglets whose mother had died. Mali's owner, the landlord of (would you believe) the Pig and Whistle pub at Privett in Hampshire, reckons she's really saved their bacon. The St Bernard, who's aged two and still waiting for her first puppies, obviously thought she'd like to sample that mothering feeling. The small herd of porkers nuzzle away happily – they look as though they're hunting for some mother's milk, but perhaps all they're really after is the brandy!

At another pub – the Blue Ball Inn at Twiscombe near Taunton – they've found a good way of pulling the birds. A goose called Twiddle-dee has taken to turning up round about opening time looking not for his regular supper, but for a pint of the usual. And that means a mug of best West Country cider. Now the ducks have waddled in on the act – matching him pint for pint.

An Italian homing pigeon entered for a 320-mile race made certain he got the wooden spoon. His flying time for the routine journey was just three years and eight months. That's ten feet every minute. He must have walked!

One night on *News At Ten* we reported that a pigeon had become a world record-holder. He'd set off on a race from Penzance to Manchester, and had ended up 6,000 miles away near Halifax, Nova Scotia. The next night we had to confess that we weren't so sure. A quite impeccable source informed us that a pigeon answering this one's description had hitched a lift on the Royal Yacht *Britannia* as it was passing Penzance en route for a Royal Tour of Canada. The crew nicknamed him Percy, gave him a comfortable cage, fed him on beer and ship's biscuits, and watched him fly away – you've guessed – off Halifax, Nova Scotia. Nice try, Percy!

For years, airports have been trying to solve the problem of how to keep birds off their runways. Liverpool hit on the idea of touring the tarmac just before landings or takeoffs with a van blaring out pop music from its loudspeakers. Not any old pop music, you understand – just Shirley Bassey! It seemed they tried all the other artists, but our Shirl was the only one to get the birds going. Let's hope she got royalties.

Towser, a tortoiseshell cat, got the mice going at the Scottish distillery she patrolled. In the course of 21 years she caught a record 23,000 mice – an average of three a day. To celebrate, her owners provided her with some food that wasn't on four legs – a 21st birthday cake. Towser munched away contentedly. What mice were left breathed a sigh of relief and watched from a discreet distance. That's one distillery where having a nip or two doesn't mean quite what you think.

The owner of Casper, a tom cat, did the right thing when he decided to move house. Casper was reluctant to go because he'd fallen in love with two Persians down the road. So Chris Sear advertised his Georgian-style home in Devon complete with Casper

as a sitting tenant. The asking price? £40,000. There was no shortage
of interest – but people did ask if he wanted a special claws written
into the contract.

Marmaduke Gingerbits, a tomcat who led something of a
double life, had his future decided by a court of law. Police Constable
John Sewell and his wife Anna said he belonged to them. Monty
Cohen, who lived in the same street at Woodford Bridge in Essex,
claimed the cat's real name was Sonny, and he was his. After a nine-
month legal battle, the dispute ended up in Bow County Court with
Marmaduke – or was it Sonny? – being cared for in police custody at
a cost of £1.40 a day. The key evidence came from the Sewells – they
claimed their cat had an allergy to milk. The RSPCA went into the
witness-box to confirm that this was so. The court duly ruled that the
cat before them was indeed Marmaduke Gingerbits. When last seen
he was being hustled into a car with a blanket over his cage to be
rushed through the hordes of photographers waiting at the gates. A
national newspaper had bought Marmaduke's exclusive story – the
claws were out in Fleet street again.

In the De Lorean trial in Los Angeles the jury was out before
the case had even begun. The court was adjourned because so many
officials wanted to watch the first baseball game of the season. The
judge didn't find it a difficult decision. It turned out he was a baseball
fan too.

Another decision came just as easily in a magistrates' court at
Lisburn in Northern Ireland. A youth aged 17 was found guilty of
causing £230 worth of damage with graffiti. The court heard the
police had no difficulty in tracing Ronald Bleakley because he signed
the graffiti with his own name. Then he had second thoughts and
tried to erase his name using bleach. But that failed. Kilroy had
better look to his laurels!

Greater artistic success is claimed by a German Prince who is
making a mint in the art world of Miami. Prince Jürgen von Anhalt's
technique is to line up a huge blank canvas behind one of the engines

Left *Marmaduke Gingerbits*, above *Monty Cohen*, below *John and Anna Sewell*.

of a jumbo jet. He then has the engine switched on, picks up pots of paint in a carefully predetermined sequence and hurls them up into the jet-stream of the engine. The paint is then whipped in a random and unpredictable way onto the canvas where it forms what the Prince claims are "unique" patterns. Hiring a Boeing in the name of art does push up the price of the finished work – but at least it proves you can make a big splash with a lot of hot air.

A farmer in Wiltshire thinks his cows have helped him lick his problem of baldness. He was bending down to pick something up in the farmyard one day when his favourite cow licked his bald pate. She seemed to like it – so, although her tongue was a bit like sandpaper, he let her do it again. To his amazement, his hair started growing once more. The word spread, and before long all his bald neighbours were turning up to have their heads licked.

It is amazing how animals can help solve human problems. The humans on the *Dallas Morning News* were so bad at tipping the winners of football matches that their editor told them even an ape could do better. So they called in Canda, a lowland gorilla from the local zoo, for a few weeks' trial in the job. Tickets with the names of teams written on them were held up in front of him – and a hairy fist made its crude selection. No fewer than ten of the fourteen teams he picked won their games – including a few real underdogs. The *Dallas Morning News* sports desk swallowed its pride. "It proves," they said, "that anyone can make a monkey out of us."

Having made it our business to reveal to the nation's news "groupies" the oddities, blunders and boobs of others, it seemed only fair not to hide an embarrassing moment when the tables were turned – and *News At Ten* found itself the victim of its own tailpiece. The programme opens every night with a picture of the earth taken from a satellite. After a second, the earth disappears – replaced by the letters ITN, and the fast-moving title sequence takes over. It's hardly enough time to take a good look at the earth – but we'd reckoned without the eagle eyes of Dr John Townshend of the Department of Geography at the University of Reading.

He wrote in to say we were showing the earth the wrong way round. This was how he put it: "Given your undoubted accuracy in reporting facts, could you ensure West Africa appears on the left of my screen and East Africa on the right? Even Continental Drift could not impose the distortion your picture creates!" We checked, and – do you know – he was right! Over 500 programmes to heaven knows how many million viewers, and no-one, apart from Dr Townshend, had noticed that the transparency was back to front. All 25 versions of the opening titles were immediately changed to rectify the mistake, giving us a chance to prove that ITN really does move heaven and earth to get it right!

And finally, I'm happy to report that there is at least one sense in which this book does *not* live up to its title. There'll be more "And Finallys" most nights on *News At Ten* – and on most of ITN's other daily news programmes too.

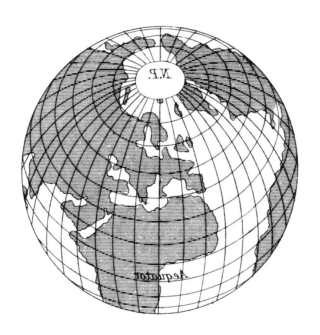

ACKNOWLEDGMENTS

My warmest thanks go
TO the ITN News Information Department, especially Doug Fenner
and Stuart Maskell, for delving into the dustiest corners to dig out the
original scripts,
TO the news editors and copy tasters in ITN and the ITV regional
companies, whose daily contacts and careful combing of agency
tapes provided such a rich harvest,
TO the producers, whose good sense and judgment (or not, as the
case may be) led to the stories being included in *News At Ten*,
TO my friends, colleagues and predecessors among the newscasters
and writers who fashioned many of the original words, but most of all
TO those splendid, wonderful people and animals whose deeds,
mistakes, disasters and eccentricities created such a rich harvest of
havoc and humour. Long may they continue to make the world more
fun for the rest of us, and to help us end *News At Ten* with a smile.